Step into R

Tom the TV Cat

By Joan Heilbroner

Illustrated by Sal Murdocca

A Step 2 Book

Corgi Books

For Peter and Annie
and their wonderful
Lolo

Series Advisor: Cliff Moon M.Ed., Senior Lecturer in the Teaching of Reading
Step into Reading™: Tom the TV Cat
A Corgi Book 0 552 523291
First published in Great Britain by Corgi Books 1986

Step into Reading is a trademark of Random House, Inc.
and is used by Corgi Books under license.
Corgi Books are published by Transworld Publishers Ltd.,
61-63 Uxbridge Road, Ealing, London W5 5SA.

Tom was a cat.

He lived in the city.

He lived at the end of Fish Street.

Tom worked for the fish man.

He did the house work.

He did the mouse work.

He did a little fish work too.

Tom was a good cat.

He worked hard.

He made the fish man happy.

One day the fish man got a box.

The box had ears.

The box made a noise.

And there were people
in the box!

Tom liked that box.

He could not stop looking at it.

He forgot about the house work…

and the mouse work…

and the fish work too.

Tom forgot all about work.

The fish man was not happy.
He told Tom to go back to work.
But Tom just went on looking
at that box.

Tom saw a man in the box.

The man was singing a song.

He sang about the moon.

He sang about the stars.

He sang about love.

People loved to hear
that man sing.
They clapped and cheered.
And ladies threw flowers
at him.

Tom wished he could sing
like that man.
He wished a lady would throw flowers
at him.

That night Tom went out.

He stood on a wall and he sang.

He sang about the moon.

He sang about the stars.

He sang about love.

He sang about fish.

Tom sang about everything
he loved.

"Meow! Meow! Meowl!
Howl! Yowl! Meowl!"
he sang.

Tom woke up the lady next door.

She threw him some flowers…

and the flower pot too.
Crash! Bang!
"Meow! Meow! Ow!"
cried Tom.
Tom did not want to be
a song cat anymore.

But he did not stop looking
at that box.

Tom saw a new man in the box.

He was not a song man.

He was a strong man.

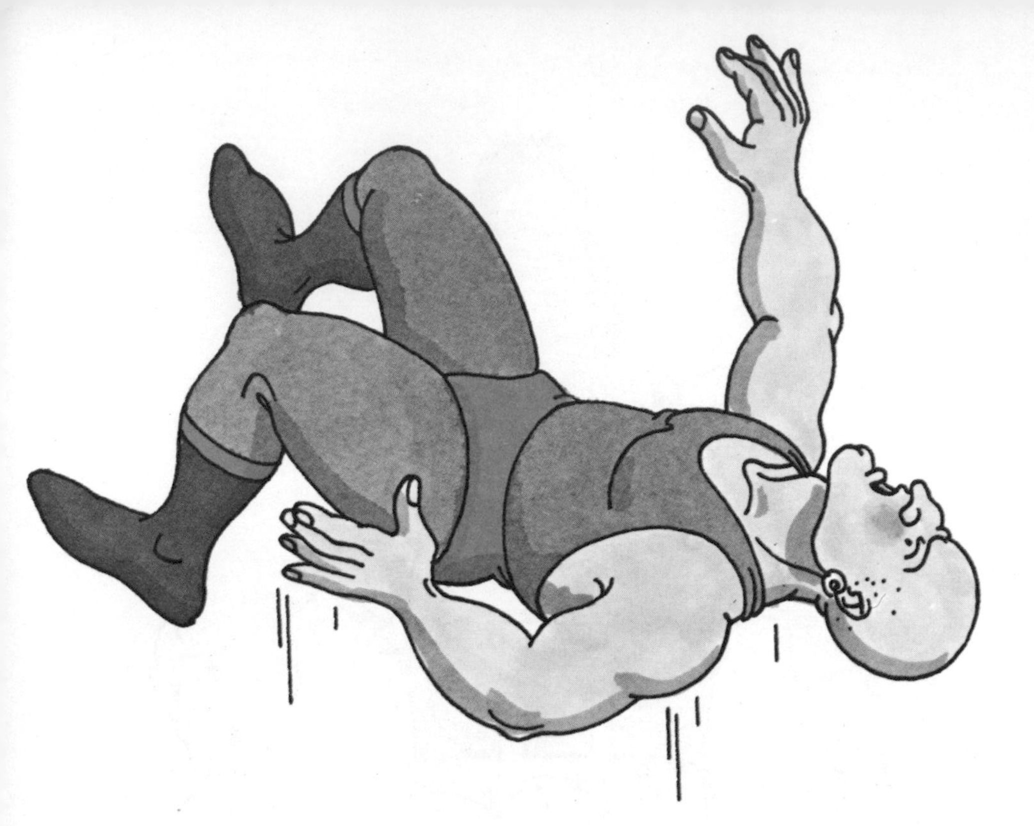

The strong man picked someone up.

He threw him up high!

Tom wished he could be strong
like that.
He wished he could throw
someone up high.

That night Tom went out.

He looked for someone to throw.

He looked up Fish Street.

He looked down Fish Street.

There was no one around.

Then Tom saw something!

It was a cat.

A big cat!

He was looking right at Tom.

Tom went over to the cat.

He looked at the cat.

The cat looked at Tom.

And then...

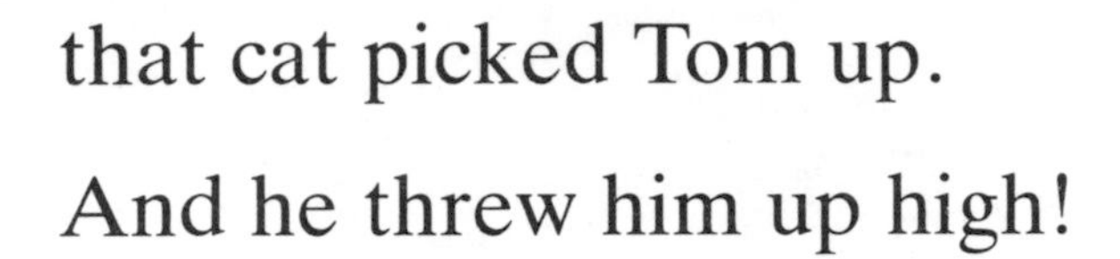

that cat picked Tom up.
And he threw him up high!

"Meow! Meow! Meow!"
yelled Tom.
"Ow! Ow! Ow!"

Tom woke up the lady next door.

Tom woke up the man next door.

He woke up the fish man too.

The lady threw some flowers.

The man threw some shoes.

The fish man threw Tom
back into the house.
"Now be a good cat,"
said the fish man.

Tom did try to be good.

He did some fish work.

He did some dish work.

And he stayed away from

that box.

But one night the fish man
went out.
Tom was all alone.
He thought about that box.
He thought he would take
just one look.

Tom did not see the song man.
He did not see the strong man.
He saw a man who made his eyes
pop out!

This man picked up a car...

and jumped over a house!

Then this wonderful man flew!

Tom wished he could fly.

He thought he would try.

Tom went up to the roof.

He put out his arms.

And he flew!

Tom flew by windows.

He flew by clothes.

He flew right into the dustbin.

"Meow! Meow! Meow!

Ow! Ow! Ow!"

he yelled.

Tom woke up the lady next door.
He woke up the man next door.
He woke up all the people
on Fish Street.

And they all threw things at him.

Tom did not want to be
a flying cat anymore.

The next day Tom went back to work.

That night the fish man looked
at the ball game.
And Tom looked too.

Tom liked the ball game.
He liked the man
who ran with the ball.
Tom wished that he could run
with a ball like that.

But then Tom saw something
that he did not like.
All the ball players were on top
of the man with the ball!

Tom closed his eyes.

He did not want to be a ball cat …

or a flying cat …

or a strong cat …

or a song cat.

Tom just wanted to be

a good fish cat.